LITTLE MISS HELPFUL
and the green house

Original concept by Roger Hargreaves
Illustrated and written by Adam Hargreaves

With a name like Helpful you would think that Little Miss Helpful would be helpful, wouldn't you?

Well, you'd be wrong.

She wanted to help people more than anything else in the world, but as hard as she tried she always ended up being unhelpful.

One day, about a week ago, Little Miss Helpful was sitting on a bus on her way to town.

Mr Slow and Mr Happy were sitting in front of her having a conversation.

"I ... wish ... I ... had ... a ... green ... house ... but ... I ... never ... get ... the ... time ... to ... do ... anything," said Mr Slow to Mr Happy.

It was a very slow conversation.

Just then the bus stopped.

Now what Little Miss Helpful had just overheard had given her an idea.

She got off the bus.

And walked across to Mr Nail's Hardware store, and bought all the green paint that he had.

Then Mr Nail delivered all the green paint to ... Mr Slow's house.

I am sure you can guess what she had in mind. That's right.

She was going to surprise Mr Slow by helping him paint his house green.

Helpful Little Miss Helpful!

Little Miss Helpful started to paint.

She painted all the walls.

She painted all the doors.

She painted the chimney and the roof!

She even painted all the windows.

The window panes as well as the frames!

When she had finished painting the house she still had some paint left over.

So she painted the garage as well.

Outside and inside!

Little Miss Helpful was terribly pleased with herself.

She stood back to admire her handiwork.

It was then that Mr Slow arrived back home.

In the time it had taken Miss Helpful to paint his house he had bought a loaf of bread.

He isn't called Mr Slow for nothing.

Mr Slow had to look twice before he realised that his house was still there.

"What ... have ... you ... done?" he exclaimed.

"You said that you wanted a green house," said Miss Helpful, "so there you are."

"That's ... not ... what ... I ... meant. I ... want ... a ... greenhouse," said Mr Slow.

"Exactly," said Miss Helpful. "And I painted your house green."

"No I ... want ... the ... sort ... of ... greenhouse ... that ... you ... grow ... tomatoes ... in," explained Mr Slow, slowly.

"Oh ... " said Little Miss Helpful.

" ... then what colour did you want your house to be?"

Mr Slow groaned a very slow groan. He could see it was going to be a very long afternoon.

Even for him!

3 Great Offers for MR. MEN Fans!

MR.MEN TOKEN

1 New Mr. Men or Little Miss Library Bus Presentation Cases

A brand new stronger, roomier school bus library box, with sturdy carrying handle and stay-closed fasteners.

The full colour, wipe-clean boxes make a great home for your full collection.

They're just £5.99 inc P&P and free bookmark!

☐ MR. MEN   ☐ LITTLE MISS (please tick and order overleaf)

2 Door Hangers and Posters

In every Mr. Men and Little Miss book like this one, you will find a special token. Collect 6 tokens and we will send you a brilliant Mr. Men or Little Miss poster and a Mr. Men or Little Miss double sided full colour bedroom door hanger of your choice. Simply tick your choice in the list and tape a 50p coin for your two items to this page.

PLEASE STICK YOUR 50P COIN HERE

Door Hangers (please tick)
☐ Mr. Nosey & Mr. Muddle
☐ Mr. Slow & Mr. Busy
☐ Mr. Messy & Mr. Quiet
☐ Mr. Perfect & Mr. Forgetful
☐ Little Miss Fun & Little Miss Late
☐ Little Miss Helpful & Little Miss Tidy
☐ Little Miss Busy & Little Miss Brainy
☐ Little Miss Star & Little Miss Fun

Posters (please tick)
☐ MR. MEN
☐ LITTLE MISS

CUT ALONG DOTTED LINE AND RETURN THIS WHOLE PAGE

3 Sixteen Beautiful Fridge Magnets – any 2 for £2.00! inc.P&P

They're very special collector's items!
Simply tick your first and second* choices from the list below of any 2 characters!

1st Choice

- Mr. Happy
- Mr. Lazy
- Mr. Topsy-Turvy
- Mr. Bounce
- Mr. Small
- Mr. Snow
- Mr. Wrong

- Mr. Daydream
- Mr. Tickle
- Mr. Greedy
- Mr. Funny
- Little Miss Giggles
- Little Miss Splendid
- Little Miss Naughty
- Little Miss Sunshine

2nd Choice

- Mr. Happy
- Mr. Lazy
- Mr. Topsy-Turvy
- Mr. Bounce
- Mr. Small
- Mr. Snow
- Mr. Wrong

- Mr. Daydream
- Mr. Tickle
- Mr. Greedy
- Mr. Funny
- Little Miss Giggles
- Little Miss Splendid
- Little Miss Naughty
- Little Miss Sunshine

*Only in case your first choice is out of stock.

--- TO BE COMPLETED BY AN ADULT ---

To apply for any of these great offers, ask an adult to complete the coupon below and send it with the appropriate payment and tokens, if needed, to MR. MEN OFFERS, PO BOX 7, MANCHESTER M19 2HD

☐ Please send ____ Mr. Men Library case(s) and/or ____ Little Miss Library case(s) at £5.99 each inc P&P

☐ Please send a poster and door hanger as selected overleaf. I enclose six tokens plus a 50p coin for P&P

☐ Please send me ____ pair(s) of Mr. Men/Little Miss fridge magnets, as selected above at £2.00 inc P&P

Fan's Name _____

Address _____

_____ **Postcode** _____

Date of Birth _____

Name of Parent/Guardian _____

Total amount enclosed £ _____

☐ **I enclose a cheque/postal order payable to Egmont Books Limited**

☐ **Please charge my MasterCard/Visa/Amex/Switch or Delta account** (delete as appropriate)

Card Number

Expiry date ___ / ___   **Signature** _____

Please allow 28 days for delivery. We reserve the right to change the terms of this offer at any time but we offer a 14 day money back guarantee. This does not affect your statutory rights.

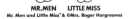

MR.MEN   LITTLE MISS
Mr. Men and Little Miss™ & ©Mrs. Roger Hargreaves

CUT ALONG DOTTED LINE AND RETURN THIS WHOLE PAGE